Lilah in the Land of The Littles

A Story for Children in the Time of Covid

Written and illustrated by Lesley Koplow

Lilah was little.

She was smaller than her brother, who was almost a teenager.

She was smaller than her sister, who was almost a grown up!

Lilah was little, but she was exactly the same age as her neighbor Jasmine. Before the Coronavirus changed everything, Lilah and Jasmine walked to school together.

Before the Coronavirus changed everything, Lilah and Jasmine played in the park together.

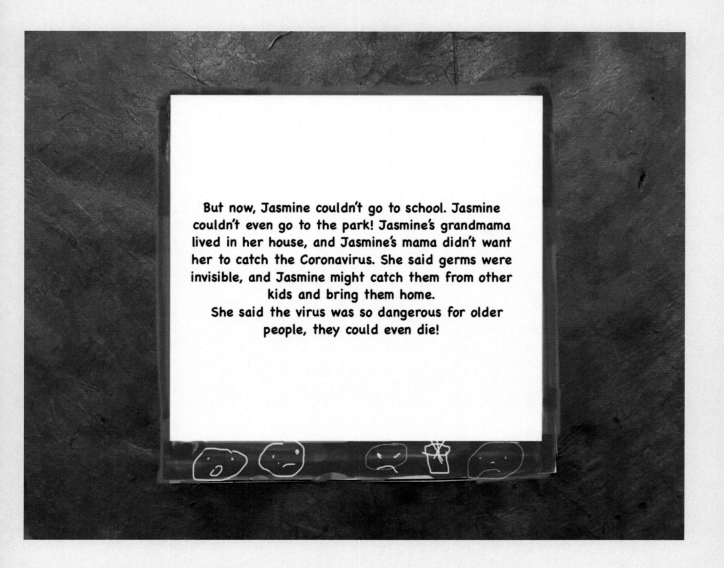

But now, Jasmine couldn't go to school. Jasmine couldn't even go to the park! Jasmine's grandmama lived in her house, and Jasmine's mama didn't want her to catch the Coronavirus. She said germs were invisible, and Jasmine might catch them from other kids and bring them home.
She said the virus was so dangerous for older people, they could even die!

"Stupid Coronavirus", mumbled Lilah. "You are the worst virus in the whole world!"

Lilah scribbled on a crinkly paper with her gray crayon.

The Coronavirus made grown-ups worried and grumpy. It made school be open only 2 days a week. It even cancelled Lilah's birthday party right before her birthday!

"I HATE the Coronavirus!" Lilah told her mom. "There's nothing to do! There's no school. Jasmine can't play. I never get to use the computers or the phone! " Lilah tore her scribbled virus into pieces and threw them everywhere!

Lilah's mother looked at Lilah who had thrown herself on the kitchen floor. She sat thinking for a moment.

"I have something you can do!" she said. "Stay here. I'll be right back."

10

When Lilah's mom came back, she had a cup full of buttons in one hand and a basket full of cloth in the other hand. "Here", she said, handing them to Lilah. "Nana gave me these to play with when I was little."

"What am I supposed to do with these?" asked Lilah?
"You'll see," said her mom.
"But I…….."The phone rang.
Lilah's mom got too basy with work to answer Lilah's questions.

Lilah stomped off with her cup and her basket, looking
for a place to explore them.

Lilah's brother was doing Zoom school in the dining room. Lilah's sister was doing Zoom school in their bedroom. Lilah's toys were all over the floor in the hallway.
Lilah's mom was on her work calls in the living room.

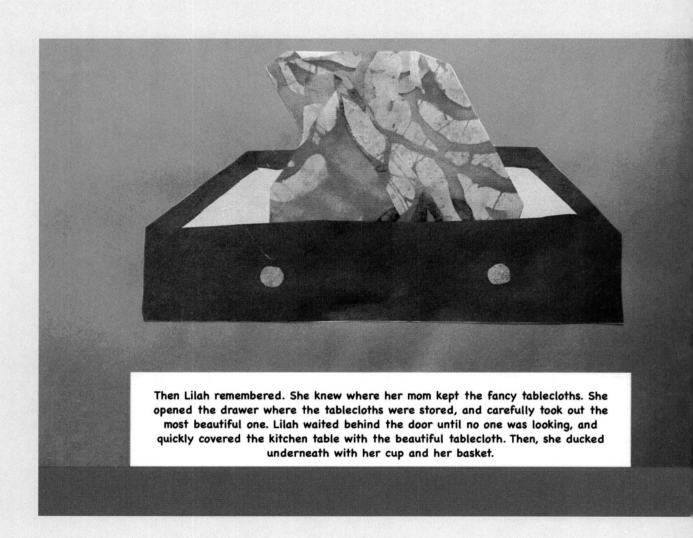

Then Lilah remembered. She knew where her mom kept the fancy tablecloths. She opened the drawer where the tablecloths were stored, and carefully took out the most beautiful one. Lilah waited behind the door until no one was looking, and quickly covered the kitchen table with the beautiful tablecloth. Then, she ducked underneath with her cup and her basket.

Now Lilah had her very own space, surrounded by giant tablecloth flowers! Lilah poured the buttons from the cup, letting them spill onto the floor like a waterfall. She looked at them as they landed. Some buttons seemed to look back at her with their button hole eyes. "You will be The Littles," Lilah whispered. "And this," she said, waving her hand over everything, will be The Land of The Littles."

There were no teenagers in The Land of The Littles. "Teenagers are too boring!" Lilah told The Littles. "They wear headphones and they can't even hear you!" The Littles understood. No teenagers allowed!

The Land of The Littles was invented in just one day. First, there was a road....

That led to another road.........

That led to a lot of houses.........

That led to a forest.........

That led to a sparkling lake.

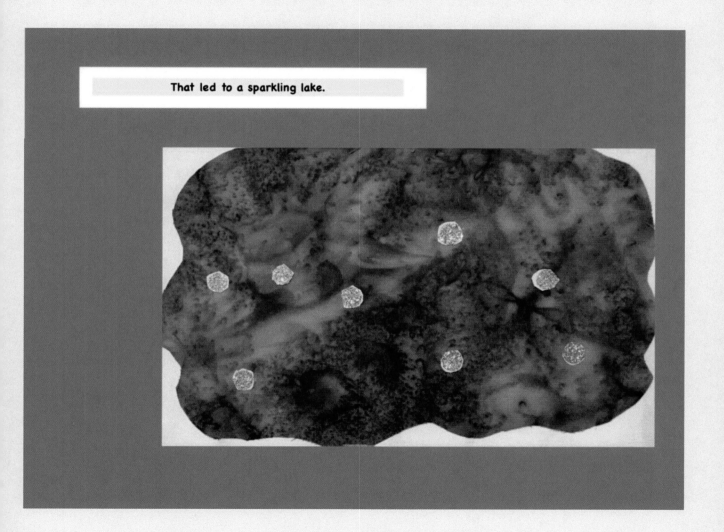

The Littles started to explore their land. They walked around without masks, because Lilah had added a magic ingrediant to the flowers that bordered their town. These flowers smelled sweet, but were poisonous to the Coronavirus!

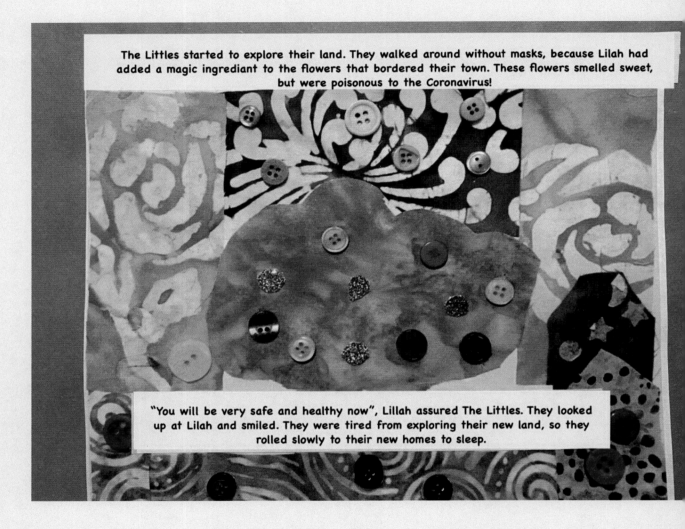

"You will be very safe and healthy now", Lillah assured The Littles. They looked up at Lilah and smiled. They were tired from exploring their new land, so they rolled slowly to their new homes to sleep.

Lilah was sleepy too. She decided to have a sleepover with The Littles. She ran to her room, changed into pajamas, grabbed her pillow and blanket, ducked under the tablecloth and fell asleep in The Land of The Littles.

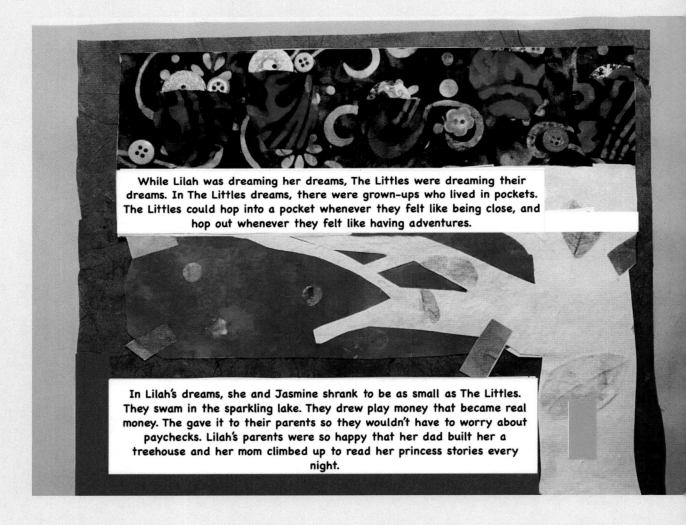

While Lilah was dreaming her dreams, The Littles were dreaming their dreams. In The Littles dreams, there were grown-ups who lived in pockets. The Littles could hop into a pocket whenever they felt like being close, and hop out whenever they felt like having adventures.

In Lilah's dreams, she and Jasmine shrank to be as small as The Littles. They swam in the sparkling lake. They drew play money that became real money. The gave it to their parents so they wouldn't have to worry about paychecks. Lilah's parents were so happy that her dad built her a treehouse and her mom climbed up to read her princess stories every night.

Since The Littles' dream pictures were close to Lilah's dream pictures, some of the images from their dreams started to overlap with the images in Lilah's dreams. Together, they created the most magical place in the universe.

When Lilah woke up, she was surprised to see Jasmine! Lilah blinked her eyes. "Get dressed!" said Jasmine. My mama said we could play outside. My grandmama went to stay with my auntie for 3 whole weeks!" Lilah jumped up. She started to hug Jasmine, but then she remembered that only The Littles didn't have to be careful. "OK! I'm getting my clothes and my mask with the stars on it!" Lilah ran to get dressed.

Lilah and Jasmine played outside. They jumped rope. They drew with colored chalk. They played hopscotch. They ate sandwiches and drank cups of iced tea sitting on the stoop, 6 steps apart.

"We can play again tomorrow!" Jasmine said happily. Lilah shook her head. " I have school tomorrow."

Jasmine looked sad. "Hey! I know something you can do while I'm at school." Lilah said. "Close your eyes! I'll be right back."

Lilah ran inside to The Land of The Littles. She took some buttons from the floor. She took some extra cloth from the basket. She put everything into a bag. "Mom!" she called. "I'm sharing some of Nana's things with Jasmine. O.K.?"

Lilah's mom nodded. She was busy getting dinner ready. Lilah was panting when she got back to Jasmine's stoop. "Here", she said, handing Jasmine the bag.

Jasmine opened her eyes and peeked into the bag. "What can I do with these?" she asked Lilah.

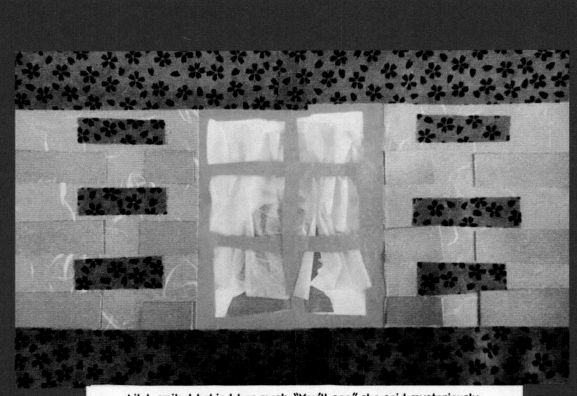

Lilah smiled behind her mask. "You'll see," she said mysteriously.
"But I......" Jasmine started.
"Lilah! Dinner!" her mom called from the window.
Lilah waved good-bye to Jasmine and ran home.

Lilah smiled as she sat down to dinner with her family. She knew Jasmine would make something wonderful.